Love Blooms

Love Blooms

A SHORT STORY

NANCY SPRINGS MORRIS

Books may be purchased in bulk quantity and/or special sales by contacting the publisher.

Published by Mynd Matters Publishing
715 Peachtree Street NE
Suites 100 & 200
Atlanta, GA 30308

www.myndmatterspublishing.com

ISBN: 978-1-957092-47-8 (pbk)

FIRST EDITION

To my beloved mother,
Ada Lucille Erwin Springs, whose grace, beauty, soft-spoken and
strong faith I so admired and try to emulate. She lovingly shared her
love story of the late 1930s when I asked,
"How did you and Dad meet?"

To my beloved father,
Zacharias Alexander Springs, Sr., whose sense of wit, intelligence,
good looks, and compassion endeared him to many. He discovered
at age eighteen true love and boldly asked my mother,
"Will you marry me?"

The courtship started with candy kisses from the hardware store and
a recitation of, How Do I Love Thee? by Elizabeth Barrett
Browning. They enjoyed sixty-seven years of wedded bliss and candy
kisses became the theme for all anniversaries and holidays.

To my beloved siblings,
Zacharias Springs, Jr., Edna Lucille Springs Laney, Erwin Springs,
Sr., Thomas Springs, Evelyn Springs, Jerry Springs, and Debbie
Ann Springs Woodson,
Our adult lives have shown our parents' desires, admiration, and
courage for hard work, compassion in reaching out to others and
remaining faithful in relationships.

Our adult lives reflect life lessons learned and taught by our beloved
parents, Zacharias Alexander Springs and Ada Lucille Erwin
Springs. As a family, we remain strong just as they taught us. We
love and care for each other just by the example they showed us. We
are active in church as they instructed us to be. We reached out to
the least of these just as they did. All glory to God for such loving
and committed parents as you.

Love Blooms

A SHORT STORY

SCHOOL

I was only twelve and a half when I met the love of my life. He was witty, smart, dark-skinned, and towered several inches above my petite five-foot-three-inch frame. We met in school when I was in the seventh grade and he was in the tenth.

In walking distance of each other, Zackary would visit every other Sunday afternoon. He appeared neatly dressed in a dark suit, a starched white shirt, and a tie. He was handsome in his Sunday hat and looked more grown up than his fifteen years.

I found myself excited as I got dressed. After he arrived, we walked to the community hardware store for candy kisses. With a bag full of kisses in hand, we ate and licked our fingers and barely talked on our way back to my house.

We talked about everything—school, baseball, and a commitment to each other as we sat on the steps of the old wooden-frame house where I lived with my mother and six siblings. My father passed away when I was seven years old.

Zachary was so much fun to be around. Sometimes, we walked down the hill just below the house and sat under a large oak tree. We would gather acorns which we would later use to fashion our initials in a clear spot on the ground (Z & L) or (L & Z). If there was more than enough gathered, we shaped a heart around the letters.

For the next two years, his visits were less frequent because of his commitment to his family, and there were always chores to be done before sunset. He also began working part-time at the golf range.

His family adored me and thought Zachary to be a lucky young man. His parents were devout Christians, and their children, including Zachary, were nurtured in the church. Prayers were said at mealtime and bedtime. His father, a prayer warrior, often prayed on bended knees at church functions, so I was told.

The summer quickly turned into fall with crisp but sunny days and a beautiful robin blue sky. The woodlands were adorned in deep browns, apple reds, and burnt oranges, and I longed to be free—from schoolwork, indoor and outdoor chores and caring for my younger siblings.

18

My oldest sister had become ill, and my mother warned me I might have to give up my schooling to help take care of her and manage the household.

"Don't expect your brothers to be much help with indoor chores," she'd say.

Zackary transferred to a new school but remained loyal to his Sunday visits. His sister, Emma Mary, continued at the same school and would deliver letters Zackary wrote to me.

He was committed to loving me no matter what and often quoted *How Do I Love Thee?* by Elizabeth Barratt Browning. He shared why he wanted a life with me.

"You are so beautiful with your long flowing black hair and fair complexion. I love your hair in a ponytail when it moves in the wind. You are so kind, and you're smart, too.

Will you marry me?
Let's elope in the spring."

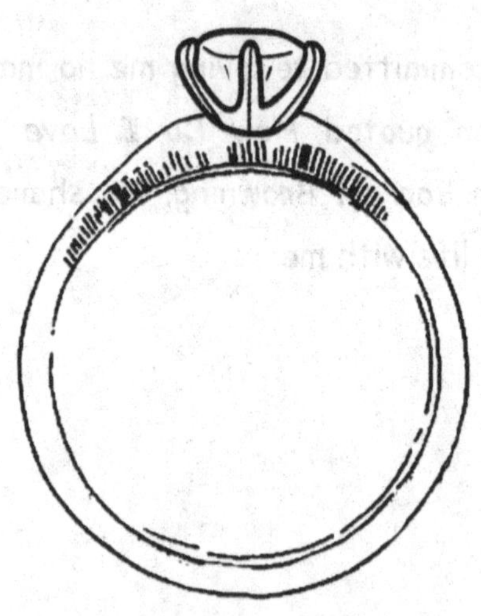

His proposal took me by surprise and my eyes shone brightly. I didn't know what to say.

He was so wise to be so young and vowed to take care of me forever. I trusted him and adored him more.

Although Zachary and I had established a strong friendship based on sharing, trust, respect, and laughter over the years, I couldn't let my mother know of our pending plans.

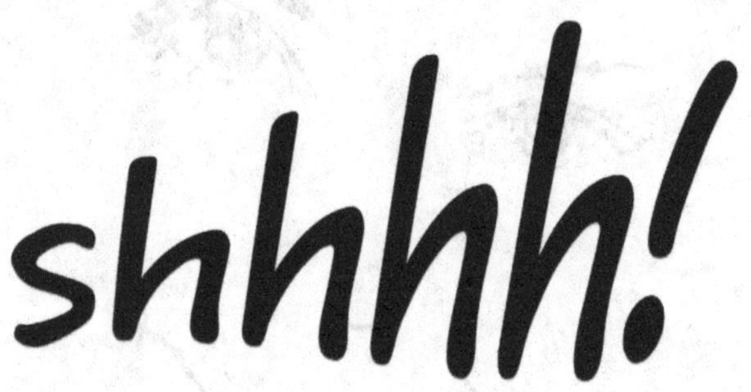

About three or four months after the new school year began, the trees lost their leaves and blue skies turned gray. Winter was nearing, and any hope of my sister's recovery was just as gloomy.

Being loyal and obedient, I did what was to be—I quit school.

Zachary and I continued to see each other on Sundays when the weather was kind. The more we were apart, the more we were drawn to each other.

We discussed more and more a commitment to each other and the plans for our elopement. I thought I would burst by keeping such a secret for so long.

The plan was to have a friend take us to the courthouse in early April. Zachary could drive but didn't have a car.

He promised to help me with my chores and offer support as I helped care for my sister and to tutor me while I was absent from school.

The winter, much milder than the one before, passed quickly and the month of April was fast approaching. April, our favorite month, would usher in color and give a reason for newness and an enthusiastic celebration.

Zachary arranged for his best friend to come for us on the first Friday of the month. I was ready and dressed as though I was going to school with a soft sweater draped around my shoulders.

After a short ride into town, we found ourselves standing in front of the judge who asked for information, including our ages. When I responded fifteen, he immediately said, "You are too young and need parental consent."

How embarrassing! We went to my mother's house and found her waiting on the front porch. Zachary tried to explain as I walked ahead towards the living room.

"You what?!" I heard from the adjoining room.

"Excuse me?! Why didn't you tell me?" she said, her voice revealing her concern and frustration. She never said a word to Zachary, just to me.

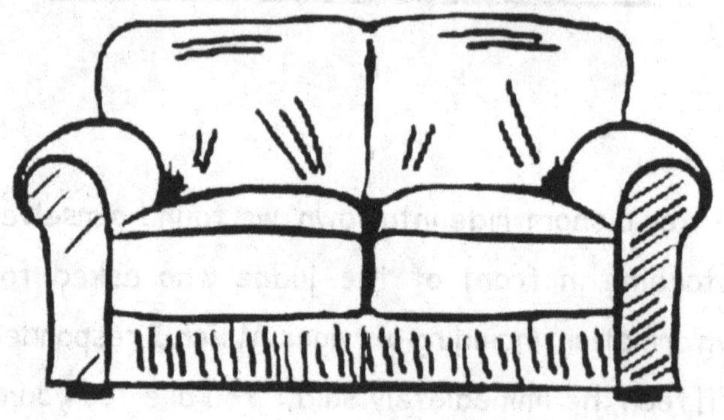

My mother found Zachary to be of strong morals and compassion, and he was indeed committed to all of us. After calming herself, she pulled the two of us together and gave us her blessing for a happy life together.

My sister, who was resting in the living room, smiled and, for the first time, glowed with a radiance I'd not seen.

Surely, this was an omen of hope for better times. I giggled with joy knowing next week I would be Mrs. Z.

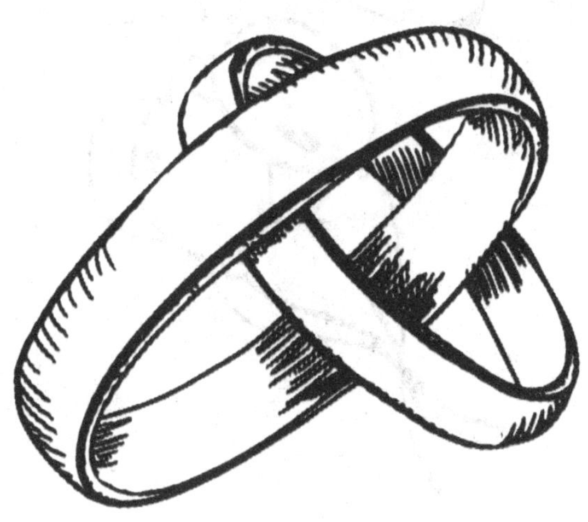

Ada Lucille Erwin Springs

Zacharias Alexander Springs, Sr.

9 781957 092478